The Consultant

Heidi Schreck

A SAMUEL FRENCH ACTING EDITION

SAMUEL
FRENCH

FOUNDED 1830

SAMUELFRENCH.COM
SAMUELFRENCH-LONDON.CO.UK

MUSIC USE NOTE

Licensees are solely responsible for obtaining formal written permission from copyright owners to use copyrighted music in the performance of this play and are strongly cautioned to do so. If no such permission is obtained by the licensee, then the licensee must use only original music that the licensee owns and controls. Licensees are solely responsible and liable for all music clearances and shall indemnify the copyright owners of the play(s) and their licensing agent, Samuel French, against any costs, expenses, losses and liabilities arising from the use of music by licensees. Please contact the appropriate music licensing authority in your territory for the rights to any incidental music.

IMPORTANT BILLING AND CREDIT REQUIREMENTS

If you have obtained performance rights to this title, please refer to your licensing agreement for important billing and credit requirements.

THE CONSULTANT was first produced by the Long Whart Theatre, in New Haven, Connecticut on January 8, 2014. The performance was directed by Kip Fagan, with sets by Andrew Boyce, costumes by Jessica Pabst, lights by Matt Frey, and composition and sound by Daniel Kluger. The Production Stage Manager was Sunneva Stapleton. The cast was as follows:

AMELIA	Clare Barron
JUN SUK	Nelson Lee
TANIA	Cassie Beck
MARK	Darren Goldstein
BARBARA	Lynne McCollough

CHARACTERS

AMELIA

JUN SUK

TANIA

MARK

BARBARA

SETTING

A pharmaceutical advertising agency in New York City.

TIME

Present, or some time shortly after the Great Recession.

AUTHOR'S NOTES

Line breaks indicate a shift in thought, and do not necessarily demand a pause. Actors should feel free to play around with the rhythms, and to make choices about punctuation.

MONDAY, FEBRUARY 2

*(The lobby of a pharmaceutical advertising company at 9 Park Avenue in Manhattan. **AMELIA**, a conspicuously young woman sits waiting next to the 8th floor reception desk. Her look is vaguely business-y, except for her cool but worn out boots. They were expensive boots at one time but now a hole is starting. She futzes self-consciously with the hole.)*

(Behind the reception desk is an aquarium-like, glassed-off conference room.)

*(The phone rings. **TANIA**, a stylishly dressed secretary in her late 30s, enters running.)*

TANIA. Sutton Feingold McGrath can you hold please
Sutton Feingold McGrath can you hold please
Sutton Feingold McGrath can you
Barbara no longer works here
Jun Suk is now handling her accounts
Jun Suk
Jun Suk
J-U-N S-U-K
I'm not allowed to give you that information.
Should I put you through to Jun Suk?

(She puts the call through.)

AMELIA. Um excuse me I'm sorry
I'm here for

(The phone beeps.)

TANIA. Hi thank you for holding
Yes he is
I'll put you through

(She presses the hold button. Looks at **AMELIA***)*

What?

AMELIA. I'm here for Jun Suk

We were supposed to meet at

(The phone beeps.)

TANIA. Hold on

(She picks up the line.)

He's not answering his phone

would you care to leave a message?

(She puts the call through. She looks at **AMELIA***.)*

You're the consultant?

AMELIA. I'm

from NYU.

TANIA. I went to NYU now look at me.

(The phone beeps.)

Hi thanks for holding

I'm sorry Barbara no longer works here

Her accounts are being

Hello?

Let me try him.

*(***TANIA** *hangs up and then presses another line. She waits and waits.)*

Hey Jun Suk you need to start picking up your phone

(She goes to hang up. She remembers **AMELIA***.)*

Also your consultant is here

Let me know if I should send her back

*(***TANIA** *hangs up. She returns to her computer. She starts typing ridiculously fast. After a bit:)*

AMELIA. …Should I just continue to wait or?

TANIA. Jun Suk has been very unreliable

Lately

It will be his undoing

(beat)

AMELIA. …Ok, well I'm fine just sitting here so

*(**TANIA** continues typing. **AMELIA** watches her admiringly.)*

(after a moment)

What was your major

TANIA. Huh

AMELIA. At NYU

You said / you

TANIA. Oh uh Comparative Lit

*(**TANIA** continues typing.)*

AMELIA. I just moved here

I'm in grad school

Public Policy with a focus on Immigration Issues

*(**MARK** enters in an awesome suit, talking on a Bluetooth. It always looks like **MARK** is talking to the air.)*

*(While talking, he somehow also manages to flirt with **TANIA**.)*

MARK. No I'm not doing it

I'm not sending him to the fucking Landmark Forum

That self-empowerment Scientology bullshit freaks me out

Yeah I don't want him trying to recruit people

Preaching all the time like that wacko Barbara it's annoying

What

No Barbara didn't get fired, she left because she started her own company.

*(He looks **AMELIA** up and down with minimal interest.)*

Yeah well I'm not sending Jun Suk there I'm handling it

No

No

We're not immune that's a myth the generics are
   killing us

Yeah maybe they can rebrand for PMS

Pre-menstrual syndrome aren't you married

Yeah it's real

Uh huh

Uh huh

Well, faith is not contrary to reason so

See you Thursday

(He hangs up.)

(to **TANIA***)* Have you seen Jun Suk?

TANIA. I thought he was in his office

   not picking up his phone again to piss me off

MARK. He's not in there

TANIA. *(re* **AMELIA***)* Well this is his consultant and she's been
   waiting for like an hour

AMELIA. well not really / an hour

MARK. Hey.

AMELIA. Hey.

MARK. Thanks for doing this

   I really hope you can help him

AMELIA. I'll do my best

MARK. *(to* **TANIA***)* You wanna come across the street

   Get some air

TANIA. I can't leave the phones anymore

   Harold disabled the answering service

MARK. What if you have to pee

TANIA. I don't know

MARK. Ok well I'll bring you something back

   You want chocolate

TANIA. Duh

MARK. Ok

*(***MARK*** exits.)*

TANIA. Do you think he's cute?

AMELIA. Oh

TANIA. I can't tell either.

AMELIA. No I mean he's a very attractive man
It's just the physical isn't paramount
(For me)

(The phone rings.)

TANIA. Sutton, Feingold and McGrath
No she's not working here anymore –
Hello?

(She hangs up.)

How old are you?

AMELIA. Twenty-two

TANIA. Jesus

(JUN SUK enters. He has a black eye. He looks like shit.)

Hey Jun Suk you have a

(JUN SUK hurries past the front desk with his head down, and exits into the office.)

(after a moment)

That was Jun Suk
He's uh

(beat)

(TANIA dials JUN SUK's number. Waits.)

Hey Jun Suk your consultant's here um

AMELIA. Amelia
Lindquist

TANIA. You have an Amelia Lindquist here to see you

(She hangs up.)

Go on back to the conference room I'll buzz the door.

(She buzzes the door. AMELIA runs to catch it before it stops buzzing.)

AMELIA. I'm sorry I didn't catch it could you

(**TANIA** *buzzes the door again.*)

(**AMELIA** *catches it just in time.*)

(**TANIA**'*s phone rings.*)

TANIA. Sutton, Feingold and

Oh hey

Barbara

How are things going with the new

Um no I don't know if Harold's in but I can

I'm not lying to you I actually don't know if he's

Well maybe he used the secret exit

Hello

(*She hangs up.*)

Wacko.

(**AMELIA** *and* **JUN SUK** *sit at a large table in the conference room.*)

(*His lunch, in a paper bag, is on the table.*)

AMELIA. So here's a discussion sheet with basic questions like

What's your name

Where were you born

The questions get more interesting in the past perfect

Have you ever been in a car accident

Have you ever had a broken heart

If the question seems too personal

You don't have to answer or you can answer

I'd Rather Not Say

JUN SUK. What

I don't

What

AMELIA. Sorry I didn't explain it well why don't we just start

What's your name

JUN SUK. Jun Suk

AMELIA. And how old are you

JUN SUK. Thirty-nine

AMELIA. Where were you born

JUN SUK. Seoul

AMELIA. Is it Seoul or Seoul

JUN SUK. Seoul

AMELIA. I've always said Seoul

JUN SUK. Seoul

AMELIA. Do you mind answering in complete sentences
    Where were you born

JUN SUK. I was born in Seoul

    *(**AMELIA** writes something.)*

    Would you like coffee
    A cup of coffee or tea

AMELIA. Oh coffee please

JUN SUK. Cream sugar

AMELIA. Just cream thank you

    *(**JUN SUK** goes to get the coffee.)*

    *(**AMELIA**'s first day is going so well.)*

    (She looks around the conference room.)

JUN SUK. You're not from Landmark are you?

AMELIA. …I'm from NYU.

JUN SUK. Ok
    I don't feel comfortable choosing the amount of cream

AMELIA. Oh here thank you
    Do you want coffee with that cream
    Ha
    Are you married

JUN SUK. No.

AMELIA. Sorry can you answer / in

JUN SUK. I am not married.

AMELIA. Where do you live

JUN SUK. Murray Hill

Is where I live

AMELIA. Great I think we can skip ahead to past perfect

Have you ever had a dream come true?

JUN SUK. ...like a prophetic dream?

AMELIA. Oh no I mean that would be way more interesting but no

Say when you were a kid you

Wanted to be an astronaut or maybe / a

JUN SUK. I dreamed of going into pharmaceutical marketing

AMELIA. Wow that's fantastic your dream came true

JUN SUK. I was joking

Wait were you joking

AMELIA. No

JUN SUK. Oh

AMELIA. You know

I have actually had a dream come true

I was born in a village and I always dreamed about living in a city

for me New York City is my dream come true

JUN SUK. You were born in a village?

AMELIA. No sorry ha no I was just born sorry in a really small town

6000 people

I have a lot of students

clients who were born in villages

Mexico or Yemen or the Dominican Republic

So I use the word Village because it creates a connection

JUN SUK. This is what psychological testing

AMELIA. No oh no gosh no

These questions help me assess your

Sorry learn about your language skills

JUN SUK. I know what assess means

AMELIA. You have an incredible vocabulary

Did you study English in Korea?

JUN SUK. What?

AMELIA. Did you study English / in

JUN SUK. No I grew up in Rye
I was a Rye Garnet

AMELIA. A what

JUN SUK. I went to Rye High
And our mascot was the Garnet

AMELIA. I'm sorry for my ignorance
But Rye is in what country?

JUN SUK. Westchester
...County New York State

AMELIA. *(shrugging)* I just moved here I'm from the West /
Coast

JUN SUK. You know that I'm American right?

(slightly paralyzed pause)

AMELIA. I thought you said you were born / in

JUN SUK. We moved to Rye when I was a baby I'm American

AMELIA. But you have a bit of an accent

JUN SUK. No I don't

(He does but it's basically imperceptible. No one but an overeager ESL teacher would say he had an accent.)

AMELIA. I mean it's very slight but
Was Korean your parents' first language?

JUN SUK. No no it's not an accent my parents spoke English
I grew up speaking English

AMELIA. Oh wow and what do your parents do

JUN SUK. Well my dad is dead thanks for asking
Why are you
Stop asking me these questions
I don't need help with my English
I need help with my personality
Apparently

Because I give shitty / presentations

AMELIA. Oh my God I'm so sorry I think I misunderstood

JUN SUK. No shit

AMELIA. I'm so / sorry!

JUN SUK. I'm supposed to be working with a presentation Coach

Or a Personality / Fixer –

AMELIA. I'm basically I'm just an ESL tutor I teach / English

JUN SUK. I think I got that

AMELIA. But I'm studying to be an Immigrant Rights Activist

JUN SUK. I'm not an immigrant!

AMELIA. No I know well I mean technically you are / but

JUN SUK. Ok you need / to go

AMELIA. I should go

I should go

thank you for the coffee

Should I wash out the / cup or

JUN SUK. Just leave / it there

AMELIA. I'll just leave it there oh god

I'm sorry I'm sorry I'm so sorry

(She gets very flustered. She is kind of flailing around.)

JUN SUK. *(softening)* Hey stop flailing around like that

AMELIA. I'm so so sorry

(He opens the door in a gentlemanly manner and gestures her out.)

JUN SUK. Worse things have happened to me

(as she's exiting:)

AMELIA. I'm so

(He closes the door.)

(He stands there for a while holding on to the doorknob.)

(Then he softly bangs his head against the door. Right where he hurt his eye.)

JUN SUK. Ow

*(He goes back to the conference table and opens his lunch. It's a peanut butter sandwich. **MARK** enters.)*

MARK. How'd it go?

JUN SUK. …

MARK. She seemed kind of young right
For a consultant
Christ what happened to your eye

JUN SUK. I got in a fight with my bathroom door

MARK.	**JUN SUK.**
Oh c'mon you can't show up with a black eye and expect me to cover for you Harold's going to flip out	It wasn't my fault. The bathroom door started it.

JUN SUK. I'll stay out of his way

MARK. I vouched for / you

JUN SUK. Jesus I get it please stop
My head is killing me

MARK. …Was the coaching helpful

JUN SUK. Oh yeah

MARK. You wanna go to Landmark instead

JUN SUK. It worked out well for Barbara

MARK. Yeah but I mean c'mon
Look
This is just a formality
You're fine you had A bad day it happens
Just suck it up and pretend like you're learning something
After the presentation we can
re-evaluate

JUN SUK. …

MARK. Those are Harold's terms

> (**JUN SUK** *can't eat any more of his sandwich. He crumples up the bag.*)

How's the situation with Maggie

JUN SUK. She gets primary custody
And now they're on vacation in Switzerland with Assface.

MARK. If you ever need to...
You know

JUN SUK. I've gotta...

> (*as he's exiting:*)

(work on Oenesta)

> (**JUN SUK** *is gone.* **MARK** *presses "1" on his phone.*)

> (**TANIA** *comes running in.*)

TANIA. Hey where's my candy?

MARK. What candy

TANIA. You forgot?

MARK. Give me a kiss

> (*on her way out*)

TANIA. Eat me Traitor

> (**MARK** *throws a chocolate at her.*)

> (*She picks up the chocolate.*)

> (*as she exits*)

I don't like Lindts

MARK. They were out of Rafaellos
THEY WERE OUT OF RAFAELLOS

> (*to the phone, tenderly*)

Hey how are you feeling?
I know I know I'm sorry things got busy
Yes but I *do* love you
Well I think I show it in my actions

> (**TANIA** *pops her head back in.*)

TANIA. Lindts

Pluh

(She spits a still wrapped-Lindt from her mouth onto the floor.)

(She disappears.)

MARK. What yes I'm here I'm here

I am listening

Uh huh

Right, but I don't know if I can do that right now

Because we laid off eight people last month, mom

Ok but you retired early so what exactly am I supposed to

(He sighs.)

Well you should have looked into the insurance stuff before you decided –

No no forget it mom I'm sorry I didn't mean

Of course you didn't plan on getting sick

I'm sorry

Mom

Mom

Mom

Look, I'll be out to visit soon I promise: I have go to Pittsburgh on business

And then I'll be out again the weekend after next.

Terrific – that sounds really fun

Hey did you get those DVDs I sent?

Yeah Becker is funny, but I think you'll like this one too

Okay well give it a chance

Bye bye

(He hangs up.)

*(At the front desk, **AMELIA** stands in front of **TANIA**'s desk. She seems agitated.)*

*(**TANIA** is still frantically typing.)*

AMELIA. I'm so sorry to bother you but I need to talk to Jun
    Suk again

TANIA. What

AMELIA. I'm

The Consultant

TANIA. Oh right

(She calls **JUN SUK**'s *line.)*

(She waits.)

Hey

Come to the lobby

Your consultant's back.

(She hangs up.)

Have a seat.

*(**MARK** enters.)*

MARK. How did he do?

AMELIA. Oh, well we just started so

MARK. Whatever you can do to help him

He's got a huge presentation coming up in a few weeks

And we just want to make sure he feels comfortable

Ok?

He's our best designer he just needs

…Body language

or

AMELIA. Sure

MARK. (Listen he had a major freakout at his last / presenta –)

*(**JUN SUK** enters.)*

Oh hey Jay your consultant's back

I'm going to go to my office

*(**MARK** exits.)*

AMELIA. I got it wrong not NYU

JUN SUK. What?

AMELIA. My resume says I do corporate coaching

I posted it on the Stern Message board I forgot

JUN SUK. …

AMELIA. I'm just saying I do have some experience working with businessmen

Mostly non-native English speakers / but

JUN SUK. I'm not a businessman I'm designer

AMELIA. Right I know I'm just saying I do have skills

I did debate in high school I won Extemp at the National Level

And in my ESL classes we do a lot of

…Performances

So I think I might have something to offer you

(beat)

(on the verge of a total meltdown) Look if you want someone else that's fine

But I'm paying my way through school

And I can't in good conscience disqualify myself from this / job

JUN SUK. Fine

AMELIA. What

JUN SUK. I have to work with someone so

AMELIA. Oh wow ok thank you thank you

Thanks a lot!

Can I give you some homework for next time

JUN SUK. No

AMELIA. Okay

See you next time

*(**AMELIA** gathers her things.)*

*(to **TANIA**) It was great to talk to you*

*(**TANIA** is still pretending not to be listening.)*

*(**AMELIA** exits.)*

(after a moment)

JUN SUK. It seems like she needs the money

TANIA. Huh

JUN SUK. That girl the consultant
I thought I should help her out

TANIA. I wasn't listening.

(**JUN SUK** *swipes his card and then turns back to* **TANIA.**)

JUN SUK. Do you have any Advil?

(*She passes him a bottle of Advil. He opens it and takes out four pills. He swallows them without water.*)

(*after a moment*)

JUN SUK. Do you know what's going on around here

TANIA. What do you mean

JUN SUK. It feels like everyone knows something
And they're not telling me

(*pause*)

TANIA. That sounds like a terrible feeling

(*pause*)

But I don't know anything.

(*She goes back to her computer.*)

(**JUN SUK** *stands there for a moment looking at her. She continues to type.*)

(*After a bit, he speaks the following in a Korean accent:*)

JUN SUK. Well thank you for the Advil

TANIA. Yeah sure

(**JUN SUK** *watches her work for a moment. Then he turns and swipes himself back into his office.*)

Hey wait I actually have to pee.
Can you

(**JUN SUK** *is gone.*)

(*She sits there.*)

FRIDAY, FEBRUARY 6

(Morning. The Lobby. **MARK** *and* **TANIA**. **TANIA** *is adjusting a little robot alarm clock. She sets it on top of her desk.)*

(The alarm goes off. The little robot clock leaps off the desk and goes running around the lobby. **TANIA** *and* **MARK** *watch it solemnly. Finally* **TANIA** *gets out from behind her desk and catches it. She turns it off.)*

MARK. Does it have a snooze button?

TANIA. No that's the whole point
you can't snooze it
you have to chase it

MARK. What if you don't feel like chasing it?

TANIA. No I will chase it I will it will drive me crazy
I don't like things that scurry

MARK. Can I borrow him for my trip?

TANIA. No I need him
I'm never going to be late again

MARK. You wanna bet on that?

TANIA. Yeah, why not. Ten bucks?

MARK. Dinner and drinks across the street. If you lose
I'll buy the dinner you just have to go with me.
That's your penalty

*(**AMELIA** enters.)*

TANIA. Hi, how can I help you?

AMELIA. I'm Jun Suk's consultant:
Amelia

MARK.	**TANIA.**
Oh hey	Oh hey I didn't recognize you.

*(**AMELIA** is dressed exactly as she was last week.)*

MARK. He called in sick

AMELIA. Oh no is he all right

TANIA. In what sense

MARK. I'm sure he's fine

He's fine

We'll have him call you to reschedule

AMELIA. Ok thanks that's actually great

I have to finish a ton of reading so I'm a little overwhelmed anyway

*(**MARK** and **TANIA** just look at her.)*

Today

MARK. Ok

Well we'll have him call you

AMELIA. Tell him I hope he feels better

MARK. Ok will do

(She exits.)

(beat)

TANIA. Just drinks

MARK. What why

TANIA. Dinner is a date

MARK. Yeah but drinks with no food:

We just end up getting wasted and

I don't know fucking in the bathroom, right?

(big charged pause)

TANIA. I should get back to work

MARK. I'm sorry that was

TANIA. I'll meet you across the street at 6:15

MARK. What oh uh

TANIA. Do you have plans

MARK. No no I don't

I don't have anything

That's great that's

(He stands looking at her. She is typing furiously.)

MONDAY, FEBRUARY 9

(In the conference room, **JUN SUK** *and* **AMELIA** *stand facing each other.)*

AMELIA. So first (you probably already know this)
  when the client enters the room you want to be confident:
  look the client in the eye
  So let's shake hands and you look me in the eye

  (Beat. **JUN SUK** *starts laughing.)*

JUN SUK. Oh wait you're serious

AMELIA. Yes

  (She puts out her hand. After a second, he grabs it. He starts giggling.)

JUN SUK. Jesus you have a vice-like grip

AMELIA. Ha thanks I'm sorry my palms are a little sweaty
  So uh now we sit down
  The book says you preferably want to put a corner
  Between yourself and your client.

JUN SUK. You're doing this from a book?

AMELIA. Um, yes it says that you should create suspense
  By leaving your drafts in your portfolio for a few moments
  While you make small talk (we can practice that later)

JUN SUK. Absolutely

AMELIA. So small talk small talk small talk
  And then you say "Let's take a look at what we have"
  Using the word we instead of I
  And using a palms up gesture
  This makes you look open and welcoming
  Do you mind trying it

  (Beat. **JUN SUK** *turns his palms up.)*

JUN SUK. Let's take a look at what we have.

AMELIA. Great! Now you take out your design folder
Set it between yourself and the client
Place your hands on the folder like this, palms down

(He does this.)

…and then very deliberately remove your hands like:
"I have something magical to unveil"

(He looks at her. Beat. He removes his hands from the folder.)

(reading) "What we're looking for with these designs
is to communicate compassion and reliability"

JUN SUK. Compassion

AMELIA. Or whatever it is you're trying to communicate

JUN SUK. Terror
The terror of insomnia

AMELIA. You're trying to communicate the terror / of

JUN SUK. Yes, the terror that will be cured by Oenesta
That's the drug

AMELIA. Ok, so: "What we're trying to communicate here
is the
Terror of Insomnia"
And then you lay down your first design

*(**JUN SUK** does this.)*

Now don't seek an immediate reaction from me
Give me the space and time to study it

*(**AMELIA** looks at his design.)*

(She is very quiet.)

(taking it in)

(She can't look at him.)

Is this you
Like a self-portrait?

JUN SUK. Oh I don't know
Does it look like me

AMELIA. Yes

JUN SUK. Then I guess it's me

AMELIA. And are you screaming for help…?

(beat)

JUN SUK. Yeah

Help I have Insomnia!

That's not what it will be ultimately

They come out sort of personal at first

Hey do you want to skip this and go get a drink

AMELIA. ohhh uhhhh / gaaark

JUN SUK. I'm sorry that was / inappropriate

AMELIA. No no it's fine it's fine

It's totally fine I'm just / not

JUN SUK. You know what I think I need to stop / for today

I just need to stop

AMELIA. No no I'm fine I just freaked out

but not because you're harassing me

Agh I mean

Sorry

I don't even feel harassed it's just

You're not on my side.

(beat)

JUN SUK. What?

AMELIA. Team I mean you're not on my –

I'm sorry

Team

I'm on the other / team

JUN SUK. You bat for the other team?

AMELIA. Yes

Yes

I mean I strike out a lot

But yes

JUN SUK. Oh

Good for you

(*JUN SUK's phone rings. He looks at the number, hits "Ignore."*)

JUN SUK. ...Do you have a girlfriend?

AMELIA. No I did in high school but we broke up when she left for UCLA

JUN SUK. A girlfriend in high school
The Clarity
Jesus

AMELIA. I'm trying to date now but it's so hard in this city
Even just making a friend seems like a real

(*JUN SUK's phone starts ringing again.*)

Odyssey
I mean I've only been here a couple / of months

JUN SUK. Excuse me I have to take this.

(*He answers his phone.*)

Hey, can we talk later I'm in a
What no, no that's not what we agreed to
Jesus Christ you can't just decide to
Maggie
Listen, do you mind if we talk later?
Yeah but I'm in a
Well then why do you call when you know I'm working!

(*MAGGIE has hung up. JUN SUK looks stricken.*)

AMELIA. ...Are you ok

JUN SUK. Yeah I'm fine
I just think I need to stop

AMELIA. I'm sorry / I'm so sorry

JUN SUK. Jesus it's not your fault
You need to stop saying you're sorry all the time

AMELIA. Sorry I mean Sorry
Sorry
Sorry I'm from the West Coast.

JUN SUK. That's no excuse.

AMELIA. Right, but in my own defense I think it's also a
   philosophical stance.

JUN SUK. What

AMELIA. I believe we are all on some fundamental level
   responsible for one another's suffering

JUN SUK. ...That's a lot to take on

AMELIA. Yeah.

   (beat)

JUN SUK. Look
   Amelia
   The thing is at the last
   At the presentation I fucked up I had to
   Stand
   The clients were sitting
   And I had to stand

   (beat)

AMELIA. Ok
   Well
   Then why don't you stand

JUN SUK. I uh
   I need to stop

MONDAY, FEBRUARY 16

(**TANIA** *is on the phone.*)

TANIA. Yes right but I'd still like to close my account
No you can't put that down that's not the reason
But that's not what I said
No, no it's not because of the fees:
It's because I feel that the bank is CULPABLE
What?
No, I'm not moving out of the country I said Culpable,
   not Country
C-u-l-p-a-b-l-e
I'm switching to a credit union
Because of your CULPABILITY

(**AMELIA** *enters in a brightly colored sweater.*)

I don't care if you don't have a box for it write it in!

(*He's not here yet.*)

(*back to the phone:*)

What yes
That's what I'm saying just write it in
Yes I'll hold

AMELIA. Do you think he's all right

TANIA. Who

AMELIA. Jun Suk

TANIA. There's a special ring of Hell
For guys like Jun Suk

   (*beat*)

AMELIA. What

TANIA. Like Dante's Inferno
Circle Two I think
Or maybe Circle Three I can't remember

AMELIA. Right but / what

TANIA. He was cheating on his wife the whole time
And now he's feeling sorry for himself

> because she fucking left him duh
> Good for her
> Give me a break

AMELIA. I didn't know that

TANIA. Oh yeah

> Mark told me

AMELIA. wow

TANIA. Also he asked me to clean out the fridge

> *(to the phone)*
>
> What?
> Hello?
> Yes I was trying to close
> My Account! What
> You're kidding
> You can't just write it in?
> Fine:
> I'm moving out of the country then
> NO DO NOT PUT ME ON HOLD AGAIN
> Fucking banks

AMELIA. Yeah Banks

> I would love to get a bunch of people together
> And buy some torches and
> Burn the motherfucking banks to the ground

TANIA. Wow

> Ok
>
> *(indicating the phone)*
>
> Maybe you should talk to her

AMELIA. *(giggling a little)* What No

> Wait
> Really...?

TANIA. Yeah

> Yeah tell her that

AMELIA. I can't do that!

TANIA. C'mon

  I dare you I double dare you
  Here

  (**AMELIA** *takes the receiver and puts it to her ear.*)

  (*They are both getting pretty excited.*)

  (*They are waiting.*)

  (*They are waiting:*)

AMELIA. Yes I just want to tell you that
  I'm going to get a bunch of people together
  And we are going to buy torches
  And we are going to burn the motherfucking / banks

  (**TANIA** *hangs up the phone.*)

TANIA. Oh my god what are you doing
  You can't say that
  What the fuck are you doing you can't threaten the
    bank

AMELIA. I thought that's what you wanted / me to

TANIA. I didn't think it through!
  And why did you say "we" they know my name and
    address
  They have all my money
  What if they think it's terrorism
  It's totally terrorism to threaten a bank

AMELIA. Oh my god I'm so sorry

TANIA. Calm down
  Be calm
  Be calm
  I'm gonna call her back and say
  Some stupid kid got on the phone and was playing a
    prank
  It's no big deal

AMELIA. I'm really sorry

TANIA. (*as she's dialing*) Shit shit shit shit shit

  (**JUN SUK** *and* **MARK** *enter from lunch.*)

MARK. It's bizarre it's called Chinese chalk and

apparently you just draw a line around your apartment with it

and the ants won't cross the line

JUN SUK. The ants refuse to cross the line

MARK. Yeah I guess the first few ants

Die and then the others just won't

Cross The Line

JUN SUK. Because they've seen the dead ones

MARK. Yeah I guess because they've seen the dead ones

JUN SUK. Ok but do they remember the dead bodies forever

Or do you have to do it all over again

Or do they remember

MARK.	**TANIA.**
I don't know the answer to that	Hello?
But I do know that it works	Hi yeah
It's called Chinese Chalk	I just called to close my account and my Daughter actually my friend's daughter got on the phone and played a little prank and so I hung up I'm sorry
(They are now watching **TANIA** *and listening to her conversation.)*	…Yes it's 867 948 30
	Yep that's it
	I'm actually really happy with my service And I'd like keep my account after all Yes because I'm satisfied with I what have. Oh great thank you thank you so much

(She hangs up.)

MARK. *(to* **TANIA***)* Jay has ants in his apartment

TANIA. Yuck

AMELIA. Maybe there are storyteller ants who tell the story of the Great Ant Massacre

(**JUN SUK** *looks at* **AMELIA.***)*

JUN SUK. Oh no you

AMELIA. Would you prefer to do this another day?

JUN SUK. I would prefer never to do this.

MARK. Oh c'mon

JUN SUK. Jesus kidding I'm kidding
I was kidding

(As he's swiping his card he ushers **AMELIA** *through the door.)*

(As they're exiting he mumbles to **AMELIA***:)*

(Nice sweater)

(**MARK** *lingers.)*

MARK. I forgot to get you chocolate

TANIA. Well you really don't owe me Chocolate
That's a completely Voluntary
Office Ritual

MARK. But I like bringing you chocolate

TANIA. Yeah well

(pause)

MARK. Hey I'm sorry
I'm sorry I didn't call you from the trip
I wasn't sure if / we were

TANIA. I didn't expect you to call

MARK. Right but I'm just saying

TANIA. It's not a big deal.

(pause)

MARK. You wanna go to Connolly's after work
Bud and shot special. Six bucks.

TANIA. I can't I'm

> *(beat)*

> Going to New Jersey

MARK. Oh.

> Cool.

TANIA. Yeah to visit my cousins

> *(**TANIA** goes back to work. **MARK** stands awkwardly looking at her.)*

> *(**MARK** stands there for a moment then exits. She lays her cheek down on her desk.)*

> *(The phone rings and rings and rings.)*

> *(She finally answers.)*

> Sutton and Feingold

> And also McGrath

> *(In the conference room **JUN SUK** standing in front of **AMELIA**, who sits, playing the part of the client. He is very nervous.)*

> Ok small talk small talk small talk

> Does the book give any

> Uh

> Topics or anything

AMELIA. It says you could tell a joke

> Something non-offensive

JUN SUK. I don't know any jokes.

AMELIA. All right well

> Next week I'll bring a joke book and / we can

JUN SUK. The presentation is next week.

AMELIA. Or you could share a personal anecdote or

> *(**JUN SUK** sighs.)*

> You know something funny that happened to you

> Recently

JUN SUK. Uh

Ok

I took a cab to work this morning because I was late

And when I opened the door I forgot to check the bike lane and I

Knocked this woman right off her bike

And I jumped out of the cab to

Try to help her off the ground

But she just started screaming

"Fuck you! Fuck you! You rich motherfuckers think you own this city"

and then she jumped on her bike and rode off screaming

"Fuck you! Fuck you Motherfucker!"

AMELIA. I don't think you should tell that one

JUN SUK. Maybe not.

(beat)

Ok so small talk small talk small talk

Then joke or personal anecdote but not that one and then

Uh

(He looks down at his feet.)

(He clears his throat.)

(He goes to stand up where he stood at the last presentation.)

(He exhales loudly.)

(He rubs his face with his hands.)

(A kind of panic is coming over him.)

(He looks down at his first design.)

(He can't speak.)

(He can't do it.)

AMELIA. *(playing the part of the client)* So

Tell me a little bit more about this second design

JUN SUK. I'm stuck
I'm stuck I just

(He's having a kind of panic attack.)

AMELIA. I think you're not breathing

JUN SUK. What

AMELIA. I just started taking yoga you should try it
I never noticed before how much I was holding my breath
I breathe in and then it's like everything gets stuck
So everything gets stuck inside of me
You have to keep moving
Life is / moving

JUN SUK. Oh my god you're insufferable

(beat)

*(**AMELIA** runs out of the room.)*

*(**JUN SUK** doesn't know what to do.)*

(He shuffles around as if to go after her and then gives up.)

*(After a bit **AMELIA** returns. Her eyes are red. She has clearly been crying and might cry again at any moment. She goes and sits in her spot.)*

JUN SUK. *(cont.)* I'm

(He clears his throat)

Sorry
What I said was
Wrong
I didn't mean it
I'm just in a bad mood lately

*(**AMELIA** sort of nods.)*

My son is being a jerk
He's uh not speaking to me right now
He's calling it a "speech strike"

(beat)

AMELIA. ...You have a son?

JUN SUK. *(nodding)* ...He's twelve

He's uh

He's really good at music

He's going to be in *Guys and Dolls* this weekend

(beat)

He's playing Arvide Abernathy

It's not the lead but it's key it's a key part in the musical

His character is a – well he's an uncle and

He has a big scene where he gives advice

To his Niece who is the lead

And he sings a really wonderful song about

Love

I guess you could say he's the voice of

Love

In the show

So that's a big deal

(MARK enters.)

MARK. Hey you were supposed to get those drafts to Harold
by noon

JUN SUK. Shit they're on my desk I forgot

Shit / Shit

MARK. I'll run them in they're on your / desk?

JUN SUK. No no I got it I got it!

I got it

I can get them

Fuck

(He's gone.)

(beat)

MARK. He says this is really helpful

AMELIA. Oh

Really...?

Thanks that's

Yeah I think I'm starting to figure out what he needs

MARK. Well what he needs is a vacation
　　but we don't have the bodies for that so

AMELIA. I'm sorry

MARK. Yeah what are you gonna do?
　　Three major drug patents died in December
　　The only good news is that anti-depressants were up
　　　fourteen percent last quarter

AMELIA. Wow that's I mean I don't know if great is the
　　right / word but

MARK. No it sucks but it's keeping us alive

AMELIA. Right.

MARK. It's a lot of pressure on him
　　This presentation

AMELIA. Yeah

MARK. Have you ever had to fire someone

AMELIA. No

　　(beat)

MARK. Well
　　Keep up the good work

　　*(**AMELIA** nods.)*

THURSDAY, FEBRUARY 26

(The sound of phone lines ringing. **TANIA** *sits at her desk. She has cut her hair very short like Jean Seberg in* Breathless. *She is talking on the phone and not picking up any of the other lines.)*

TANIA. It was supposed to be like Jean Seberg in *Breathless*
I thought I would feel so
Like Jean Seberg in *Breathless*
I mean before all the bad stuff happens

(She is suppressing a wild hysteria.)

I don't know
I guess I feel fucking exposed!
It's just a word, mom!
Well I can't pretend everything is okay all the time
I need to be allowed to express my

*(**AMELIA** enters.**TANIA** quickly recovers.)*

I've got to go.
I'm at work
Yes, I'm fine I'm totally fine.
I'll call you later.

(She hangs up.)

Hey

*(**AMELIA**'s face lights up at the sight of **TANIA**'s hair. She starts clapping.)*

AMELIA. Oh my god I love your hair.

TANIA. Oh, yeah, thanks.

AMELIA. It's just like Carey Mulligan!

TANIA. Just practical really
Jun Suk's not in yet

AMELIA. Oh no.

TANIA. He's hopeless

AMELIA. I think he's depressed

TANIA. Yeah well I'm pregnant, so

(beat)

AMELIA. Oh.
Wow.

TANIA. Yeah.

AMELIA. Who's the wow
Does it have a father

TANIA. Oh yes

AMELIA. Congratulations

TANIA. (It's Mark)

(beat)

(**AMELIA** *starts screaming with excitement.*)

Hey shhhhh!
C'mon calm down we're not even really
Why are you so excited?!

AMELIA. I didn't think I'd know who it was

TANIA. Well you can't
Jesus
You can't tell anyone you have to swear
Because I have no idea what I should do

AMELIA. I support whatever choice you / make

TANIA. Oh my god
What am I doing?
My cousin in Jersey always used to joke that I should just
get myself knocked up in a public bathroom
"Just get yourself knocked up in a bar bathroom –
Your mom will be so happy to have a grandchild she won't care how you did it."
So I guess that's what I did, I mean not consciously of course

AMELIA. Did you use protection?

TANIA. What
No

AMELIA. So that's kind of conscious…?

   (The phone rings.)

TANIA. Sutton, Feingold and –

   Oh Hey Harold

   No I haven't seen Jun Suk

   He's probably working from home…?

   Sure

   (She hangs up.)

   I'm so nice

   (to **AMELIA***)*

   Look I'm not an idiot

   There's no fucking way I should have been ovulating

   I mean you can accuse me of trying to get a disease

   But not of trying to get knocked / up

AMELIA. I'm sorry you ovulated / wrong or…?

TANIA. Apparently

AMELIA. And just from that one time that's / wow

TANIA. Yeah

   Yeah

   I mean we actually

   uh

   We actually spent the whole weekend together

AMELIA. Oh.

TANIA. We only really left the bed once

   On Sunday morning to go to Whole Foods

   And then we came home and he made an omelet and

   Put fresh tomatoes in it and then we watched *Chris
     Mathews*

   Oh my god Amelia

   What the hell are we doing with our lives!

   Well you're twenty-two so you don't need to know

AMELIA. I'm going to be an Immigrant Rights activist

TANIA. Really

AMELIA. Yeah I just started my PhD in Public Policy
At NYU
My plan is to work for five to seven years in Advocacy
And then eventually score myself a government appointment

TANIA. Wow

AMELIA. I already speak Spanish and I just started taking Arabic

TANIA. You're a little young to have that figured out
Don't you think

AMELIA. I don't know

TANIA. Yeah you'll see

AMELIA. Why what did you plan to do when you were young

(beat)

(**MARK** enters.)

MARK. Whoa your hair.

AMELIA. Doesn't she look just like Carey Mulligan!

MARK. *(unconvinced)* What, oh
yeah

(beat)

Watcha girls
Doing?
Talking?
Girl Talk?

AMELIA. Yeah girl talk
Like on *The View*

MARK. Heh

TANIA. Actually I'm not uh
I'm not feeling very well
I'm a little
I think I need some air
Amelia – *(She indicates the phone.)*
Do you mind?

(**TANIA** *is gone.*)

AMELIA. …Sure.

(*pause*)

MARK. Is she all right?

AMELIA. …

MARK. Is she depressed or

AMELIA. No, not exactly

(*beat*)

MARK. I'm gonna go out for some air too
If Harold calls
can you just say I'll be back in five minutes or so

AMELIA. Oh I don't really know how to

(*indicates the phones*)

(**MARK** *is gone.*)

(**AMELIA** *looks around at* **TANIA**'s *desk.*)

(*She sits in her chair.*)

(*She feels very grown up.*)

(*She looks at* **TANIA**'s *computer, sneaks a look around to make sure no one is watching and quickly puts on her headphones.*)

(*She can't hear anything, so she takes them off and pulls them out of the jack.*)

(*She jumps when a Pema Chodron's teeny voice is heard from the monitor:*)

"Yes, yes, and then we feel as if we're between the fingers of a big giant who is squeezing us and squeezing us. Our ideals and the reality of what's really happening / don't"

(*She shuts it off and looks around to make sure no one heard.*)

(*Suddenly* **TANIA**'s *phone rings.*)

(*And rings. And rings.*)

(AMELIA finally picks up the phone.)

AMELIA. Sutton, McGrath, and Feingold

Um no

Barbara no longer works here.

I can't tell you that.

Jun Suk.

Jun Suk.

J-U-N S-U-K

Can I transfer you to Jun Suk?

(She looks down at the phone, confused. And then pushes a couple of buttons without much conviction and quickly hangs up.)

(The phone rings again)

Sutton, Feingold, McGrath

Oh, I'm so sorry

It turns out our phone system is broke – broken

Could you call back in say an hour?

Yes, we have a man coming in to fix the system – "Doug"

Yes, Doug will have everything up and running within the hour

Thank you for calling

(She hangs up.)

(BARBARA enters.)

Sutton, Feingold, McGrath

Can I help you?

BARBARA. I need to speak to Harold

Are you new?

AMELIA. …Yes.

BARBARA. Tell him Barbara wants to see him

AMELIA. Oh hi

Barbara

Barbara!

BARBARA. Hey

AMELIA. I don't know if Harold is in / but

BARBARA. You can buzz me back I know where his desk is

AMELIA. Oh I'm just filling in I don't know / how to

> (**BARBARA** *pulls a key card out of her purse.*)
>
> (*She goes to the door.*)
>
> (*She swipes herself in.*)
>
> (**AMELIA** *is worried.*)
>
> (*She tries Harold's line.*)
>
> (**BARBARA** *returns.*)

BARBARA. He's not back there Where is everybody?

AMELIA. Uh

BARBARA. Deaththroes

AMELIA. What

BARBARA. Have they fired Jun Suk yet

AMELIA. uh no no he's doing great

BARBARA. Oh c'mon
> I was there
> When he melted down
> What's your name

AMELIA. …Amelia

BARBARA. Your life can be
> Whatever you imagine it can be
> Amelia
> But you have to imagine it first

AMELIA. …What

BARBARA. I didn't know that while I was working here
> I couldn't see it
> This place is sick it's not bad it's not evil
> But it is sick
> It's not your fault you can't see it because you're buried
>   deep inside
> The Organism
> But think about it
> In a hundred years, will this building even be here

This building will probably be razed to the ground
And your grandchildren
If they tell stories about you
They won't be stories about how you
Worked as a secretary in a Pharmaceutical Advertising
    Company
I mean let's face it even if you work your way up
Become an account manager
Do you want to work your way up

AMELIA. No I don't actually / (work here)

BARBARA. You girls!
You're aiming too low
What happened?
There was a moment, when I was in my twenties
There was this golden moment
And I'm not saying you girls you frittered it away
It's not your fault I don't blame you
In fact in many ways I take responsibility
My generation I mean should take responsibility
My daughter I bought her the album *Free to Be You and
    Me*
Do you remember this album

AMELIA. No

(**AMELIA** *shakes her head no.*)

BARBARA. (*sings**) *
EVERY BOY IN THIS LAND GROWS TO BE HIS OWN MAN
IN THIS LAND EVERY GIRL GROWS TO BE HER OWN WOMAN

AMELIA. Oh / yeah

BARBARA. My daughter wore that record out
I had to buy her a new copy
My daughter
She's a teacher now, which is a very honorable
    profession obviously

---

* Please see Music Use Note on page 3

BARBARA. *(cont.)* But not what we were fighting for in the
seventies

The opportunity for women to become teachers was
not

Our goal

That would be like fighting for women to become
Nurses or

Actresses or something

Ha

Do you

Are you close with your family

AMELIA. Yes I am

Well my older brother is in the Navy

So we /don't

BARBARA. Oh God your poor mother

AMELIA. Yeah but he wanted to go

They're giving him an education

And he won't have any loans

I'm in grad school at NYU so

BARBARA. Oh Hell

AMELIA. Yeah I know it's going to be hard

to pay it all back

But I'm trying not to think about that now

BARBARA. Listen to me: Think about it now

Think about it now start thinking about it right now

The thing that happens to us Amelia

Is that we get stuck with the story we tell ourselves

It's not so much that the past haunts us

Or that we're carrying it around like a snail carries

His house on his back

It's that we make The Past

Our Future

Like you with all those loans

That's

your Future

AMELIA. Yeah but I can't do anything about that right now

BARBARA. Bullshit you've got to make money.

>   Those loans are no one's
>   Responsibility but your own

AMELIA. I do I mean I am I have

>   a plan
>   I'm going into immigration policy
>   I want to help people who are
>   Unfairly treated by / our

BARBARA. You've got what $100,000 in loans but you're

>   going to help immigrants ok
>   Are your parents in good health

AMELIA. yes

BARBARA. Well they won't be forever

>   Do they have money

AMELIA. They're high school teachers / so

BARBARA. So no

>   Who's going to help you
>   Amelia
>   You are
>   You're responsible to
>   Yourself
>   And that's it
>   That's it
>   But that's ok and you know why
>
>   *(beat)*

AMELIA. …

BARBARA. What are you doing tonight

AMELIA. Oh I don't know

BARBARA. I'm going to this seminar

>   No pressure
>   But
>   Since I started attending these courses
>   I've quit my job and started my own business

BARBARA. *(cont.)* I've made up with my daughter
She wasn't speaking to me
Now we're on the phone every day
She's coming for my birthday she's bringing
Her latest boyfriend
I make thirty percent more money than I was making
Here and I was making good money
Here
I don't have to deal with Harold any more
I'm dressing better
I know what colors look good on me
I've found a new apartment that is
Just
It's filled with light, it's near Prospect Park
I go for an hour long walk every day
I can do that because you see I make
My own schedule
I make my own life
Does that sound like something that
Would interest you...?

(The phone rings.)

AMELIA. Sorry I have to

BARBARA. Of course It's your job

AMELIA. Sutton, Feingold and McGrath
Oh well
Yes
Can you hold just a moment

(She covers the mouthpiece.)

It's for you
Do you want to

BARBARA. Sure
Harold's not here
Why not

(She picks up the receiver.)

BARBARA. *(cont.)* Hello

Hey Travis

Yeah but I actually don't work here anymore

I can yes I can give you the inside scoop on this

Shit-show here's my cell

917

You got a pencil

917-249-9897

Why don't you give me a call in half an hour

Does that work for you

Perfect

Otherwise I'm calling you

That's right

(She hangs up.)

Listen I've got to talk with this client

But before I go do you want to try something

AMELIA. …ok

BARBARA. Can you think of something traumatic that happened to you

When you were say around seven

AMELIA. I had a really happy childhood so

BARBARA. Bullshit

AMELIA. Uh

Ok well

*(**AMELIA** thinks.)*

When I was in first grade

We were on a field trip to the Apple Juice Factory

And I kept asking my teacher Ms. McDougal

I kept asking her questions like

Can I have more apple juice?

And what happens to the stems?

And the seeds?

Stuff I thought they should have explained

And finally she lost it she said

AMELIA. *(cont.)* Will you just shut up Amelia!

So I just kept drinking more and more

Apple Juice

They were giving it out for free in little paper cups

And I kept drinking it to make myself feel better

And I drank so much I had to go to the bathroom but

I was too scared to ask Ms. McDougal

I was afraid that she would tell me to shut up again

And I peed my pants

And Garrett Grubb's mom had to take me home

She was very nice she snuck me out of the Apple Juice Factory

And took me home to change my clothes

(beat)

BARBARA. You were too scared to ask for what you needed

So you took revenge

You took revenge by peeing your pants

AMELIA. Oh I don't know

About

Revenge

BARBARA. Sure you did

Admit it

You pissed all over yourself

So you could take revenge on your teacher

And on top of that

You got what you needed

Someone swooped in and she cared for you

Right?

Garrett Grubb's mother

She took care of you so you didn't have to take care of yourself

So you didn't have to take responsibility for yourself and risk

Being told to Shut up

Okay

So Amelia

When you die

Do you want your tombstone to read

"Amelia was once told to shut up at an Apple Juice
Factory

And her Life has been a Revenge on that moment ever
since

The End."

(pause)

AMELIA. ...No

BARBARA. Here's my card

The first seminar tonight is free and

There's no pressure to keep coming

*(**BARBARA** exits.)*

*(**AMELIA** looks at the card.)*

*(**AMELIA** takes out her cell phone. She dials.)*

AMELIA. Hi Jun Suk this is Amelia

Listen, I hope you're ok and also:

(She takes a deep breath.)

You should let me know if you need to miss a session.

because I commute from Sunset Park.

I mean it's not terrible because the D train is express.

But I would still just really appreciate a call.

(She hangs up.)

(She goes and sits at the desk.)

*(**MARK** enters.)*

MARK. Can I ask you a question?

*(**MARK** pulls a bouquet of yellow roses from behind his
back.)*

Do these mean friendship?

Some homeless lady just told me they mean friendship
is that true?

AMELIA. I don't really know much / about

MARK. Can you look it up?

AMELIA. It's not my computer but sure.

MARK. Is Tania back yet.

AMELIA. No

MARK. Well quick before she gets back.

AMELIA. Um ok

MARK. Hurry

AMELIA. Here it is

it says

"The warm feelings associated with the yellow rose"

blah blah blah

"are akin to those shared with a true friend."

MARK. Here you can have these.

(He runs out of the building.)

*(**AMELIA** looks around for some place to put the flowers.)*

*(**JUN SUK** enters.)*

AMELIA. These are for you

They mean friendship

(beat)

JUN SUK. I'm sorry I can't accept them

AMELIA. Why not?

(He walks past her into his office.)

JUN SUK. I don't know I just can't

AMELIA. Are we still having our…?

What about your presentation tomorrow

(He's gone.)

*(**TANIA** re-enters from her walk.)*

TANIA. What are those.

AMELIA. They mean friendship.

TANIA. Well

That's the nicest thing anyone's done for me in long

time

TANIA. *(cont.)* Isn't that pathetic?

    (beat)

AMELIA. I'll go put them in water

    *(**AMELIA** exits. **TANIA** sits. She blows her nose.)*

    *(**MARK** enters with a dozen red roses.)*

MARK. These are for you

TANIA. Why is everyone getting me flowers

    Do I look sick or something?

    *(**AMELIA** enters, sees **MARK,** and goes back into the bathroom.)*

MARK. No, no, of course not I just

    I had a really great time with you

    And I don't

    I don't exactly understand why you haven't been speaking to me

    But I've tried to respect your feelings

    And I think I have respected your feelings

    Do you think I have?

TANIA. Yes, I do, actually, thank you

MARK. So I've been respecting your feelings and now

    I'd like to say my feelings if that's ok

    My feelings are

    Well

    These are red roses

    So I guess that's clear, right?

TANIA. We fucked in a bar bathroom.

MARK. Believe me I know I think about it all the time

    I mean All The Time I can't stop thinking about it

    I'm not exaggerating

    I'm thinking about it right now.

    *(**MARK** leans in to kiss her. She pulls back suddenly.)*

TANIA. Look I just

    I uh don't feel very well.

MARK. I really do like your hair.

TANIA. Please can you

    I'm not

    I feel like you're sort of trapping me behind

    This desk

    (She starts hyperventilating a little.)

MARK. Whoa are you ok

TANIA. I just I need a minute

    Can you please

    Can you please just get the fuck out of here?

    (beat)

MARK. Yeah.

    (He exits.)

    *(**AMELIA** returns.)*

AMELIA. Are you ok?

TANIA. …

AMELIA. Can I help

TANIA. I really doubt it

    *(**TANIA** blows her nose.)*

    *(She sits there. **AMELIA** doesn't know whether to leave or stay.)*

    (after a bit)

    …Do you think he seems like a good person?

AMELIA. Yes but I don't really know him

TANIA. It would be hard of course but

    We have health insurance

    And maybe if I

    If I had to come to this job because I was

    Saving money to send my daughter to college or…son

    You know whatever

    It might not be so bad

If it was for this greater good
I mean I know I'm not supposed to have
A child just to give my life purpose but
It would give my life purpose so
Why do they say that?
I mean it's not how I thought it would happen
But so far that's been true of pretty much everything
In my life so fuck it

AMELIA. Yes fuck it this is your life
It can be whatever you imagine it can be

TANIA. Yes it can
Right?

(beat)

I feel weirdly
…elated
Yeah,
Yeah I feel
…happy?
Or like
You know that dream where you discover there is an
extra room
In your apartment
it's been there all along but you just never noticed it
All this time
There's been this extra room
And you didn't even know it was / there

*(**JUN SUK** enters. He sees **AMELIA**:)*

JUN SUK. About before
I'm sorry I would just rather not meet today
I don't want to get in my head

AMELIA. That's ok
I have a good feeling about tomorrow

TANIA. Me too I have a good feeling too

JUN SUK. Really?

TANIA. I mean come on you're the best designer here
    What's not to love
    They're fucking crazy if they don't love you

JUN SUK. Oh / Well

AMELIA. Yeah they're fucking douche bags
    If they don't / love you

JUN SUK. *(deeply uncomfortable)* Okay, thanks guys

    (beat)

    I should get back to work

    (as he is swiping his card)

AMELIA. Are you sure you don't want to just try it for me
    once

    (JUN SUK *stands at the door.)*

JUN SUK. No.
    Thank you.

    (as he exits)

AMELIA. Break a leg!

TANIA. Yeah break a leg!
    Hey
    Could I
    Talk to you

MARK. Oh uh
    I've gotta get ready for tomorrow so

TANIA. Sure
    Maybe tomorrow
    After the

    (beat)

MARK. Yeah
    Tomorrow

    (He exits.)

    (AMELIA *and* **TANIA** *just sit for a moment)*

AMELIA. Would you want to go get a drink sometime?
    Go sit in a bar some time and just
    Play the jukebox?
TANIA. Oh uh
    Sure why not!
    I mean I'll have to have like an O'Doul's duh
    But
    Yeah why not

(**AMELIA** *is so pleased.*)

(*hours later:*)

(*The whole office is dark except for the conference room.*)

(**JUN SUK** *is alone, sitting at the table…*)

(*He mimes shaking hands with someone. His gaze is down. He tries it again, this time looking the person right in the eye. He gestures to the person to sit, then sits down himself, putting a corner between himself and the other person.*)

(*He opens his hands, palms up, and smiles at the other person.*)

(*He is open and welcoming.*)

(*He performs these and all subsequent actions solemnly, quietly; there is nothing performative about his business style:*)

(*The other person is talking.* **JUN SUK** *listens attentively and openly and without strain. He seems genuinely interested in what the other person has to say. He nods occasionally, smiles, but not too big.*)

(*He reaches down. There is a briefcase next to his chair. He stands and puts it on the table. He opens it. He takes out a folder and puts in on the table between himself and the other person. He shuts the briefcase. He puts it on the floor next to his chair.*)

(*He opens his hands.*)

(He places his hands on the folder, palms down. He deliberately removes his hands. He notices that they are shaking. He takes a deep breath.)

(He deliberately places his hands, palms down on the briefcase and lifts them off.)

(They are shaking.)

(He takes a deep breath.)

(He calmly puts his hands back on the briefcase.)

FRIDAY, FEBRUARY 27

*(The lobby. Afternoon. The phone is ringing and ringing on several different lines. **TANIA** comes racing in.)*

(She answers the phone.)

TANIA. Sutton, Feingold and McGrath

No I'm sorry he's not he's in a meeting all afternoon. Would you like his voicemail?

One moment please.

(She transfers the call. She digs her purse and gets out a bottle of vitamins. She takes one.)

(She turns to her computer and clicks on a page that was already up.)

*(**TANIA** stares at the computer.)*

*(**JUN SUK** and **MARK** enter. They both are wearing beautiful suits and look fantastic. They are also very tipsy. **JUN SUK** looks down at the ground. **MARK** has his arm around him.)*

TANIA. *(cont.)* Oh god oh no what happened

MARK. It was

How can I say this…

GENIUS!

Dude was a MOTHAFUCKIN/ GENIUS

JUN SUK. I WAS A MOTHAFUCKING GENIUS

TANIA. oh my god that is fucking / FANTASTIC

YES /

YES

YES

*(**JUN SUK** performs third verse of "Jump Around" by Hous of Pain, with underscoring by **TANIA** and **MARK**.*)*

TANIA. *(applauding wildly)* Congratulations Jun Suk!

This is huge this is

---

* Please see Music Use Note on page 3

TANIA. *(cont.)* Wait wait I have an idea!

Jump! Jump!

(She disappears behind the desk.)

(She reappears with a bottle of champagne that looks like it was rescued from the bottom of a ship.)

It's my End of The World Champagne

Let's / drink it

JUN SUK. Your what

MARK. Yeah / What

TANIA. *(as she's opening it)* Doesn't it look like it was rescued from an Old pirate ship

JUN SUK.	**MARK.**
Yarrr it does	Yeah it actually does
Arrgh	

(The cork pops. As she's pouring:)

JUN SUK. My friends

We truly deserve this Pirate Champagne

One of the finest pirate champagnes on the market

MARK.	**TANIA.**
We do deserve it	Hear hear!

MARK. *(to TANIA)* Especially this guy he killed it

You my friend are one charming

Motherfucker

I had forgotten just how charming you can be

JUN SUK.

How do you like me now

How do you like me now	**TANIA.**
How do you like me nooooooooooooow	We like it
How do you like me nooooooooooooooooow	

MARK & TANIA. We like it!

*(They drink. **MARK** and **JUN SUK** down their glasses,
TANIA takes a tiny sip.)*

*(as **JUN SUK** pours himself another glass)*

JUN SUK. Uh

I know I've been kind of

An asshole

These past few months

*(**TANIA** looks down.)*

And I just want to

thank you for

(beat)

MARK. Hear Hear!

*(**MARK**'s phone rings again.)*

Shit it's Harold

Hello?

Uh yeah, sure right now?

Yeah I'll be right in

(He hangs up.)

MARK.

Shit. Shit.	**JUN SUK.** *(laughing):*
Tan do you have any gum	Oh shit
Or mouthwash	Oh shit

TANIA. Um

MARK. Harold wants me see me in his office and I'm a little
Do I reek of Maker's?

TANIA. Here's some Trident
You'll be fine

MARK. Right but do I seem amped?

TANIA. Yeah a little

MARK.

No like yipped?	**TANIA.**
Can I have two pieces	Like what?

MARK. *(cont.)*

Motherfucker	**JUN SUK.** *(laughing)*
like coked up	He's been taking
do I seem	
coked up?	
Like I'm on drugs	illegal drugs
Like I've been taking	
illegal drugs	

TANIA. Well now you do, yeah

*(**JUN SUK** starts laughing.)*

MARK. Do you have some perfume or?
Oh shit I'm gonna lose my job

TANIA. You're not going to lose your job
Here uh
Here's some lavender face spray

(She starts spraying him.)

JUN SUK. I want lavender face spray!

*(**JUN SUK** suddenly gets very tired and sort of collapses back into the chair. It's clear now that he is extremely wasted.)*

TANIA.	**JUN SUK.**
He's not going to fire you after landing a big account	yeah, ok
Tell him you had one celebratory drink	
he's not a fucking puritan	
Here look at me	
You'll probably get promoted	

MARK. Shit you're right!
I'm getting promoted
We're fucking getting promoted!

(She straightens his hair.)

(He kisses her very suddenly.)

TANIA. Ok stop you're drunk.

MARK. I'm not as drunk as I've ever been.

TANIA. You're all right.

(She pats him on the back.)

MARK. Yeah. Yes. Yes, I am.

*(They watch **MARK** walk sort of unsteadily out of the office.)*

*(**JUN SUK** stares at **TANIA**.)*

TANIA. What

*(**JUN SUK** starts singing, softly, the first verse of "More I Cannot Wish You" from* Guys And Dolls.*)*

JUN SUK. Hurrrm Hurrrrm I can wish you

(beat)

I think I peed my pants.

TANIA. Oh my god I can smell it

JUN SUK. Sorry.

TANIA. Well go the bathroom and clean
Yourself up
And then get some fucking towels and
Oh my god I'm not your mother
What the hell is wrong with you
When are you going to grow up
What is this
You're like forty years old aren't you like forty

JUN SUK. …no

TANIA. You act like babies

JUN SUK. I'm thirty-nine

TANIA. I can't take it anymore what is wrong with everyone?

JUN SUK. How old are you?

TANIA. Shut up and go get some towels

---

*Please see Music Use Note on page 3

JUN SUK. I can't

TANIA. Jun Suk

Pull yourself together

You just won a huge account

JUN SUK. Yeah isn't it awesome

TANIA. Get up off of the floor right now

before someone comes out here and fires your ass

Hurry up

(**JUN SUK** *sort of stumbles to his feet and to the bathroom.*)

(**TANIA** *looks at the piss on the floor. She is not going to clean it up.*)

(*She goes to her desk and gets the lavender spray and sprays it in the air.*)

(*The phone starts ringing.*)

(**JUN SUK** *stumbles out of the bathroom.*)

JUN SUK. I need to lie down.

(*He exits.*)

TANIA. Jun Suk!

No way.

Asshole.

(*She walks to the bathroom.*)

(*She comes back with a giant ball of paper towels.*)

(*The phone is ringing and ringing.*)

(*She puts the whole pile on the pee so she doesn't have to touch it.*)

(*She mops it up with her foot.*)

(*She takes two paper towels as gloves and picks up the huge pile and throws it in the trash.*)

(*She starts spraying more lavender face spray.*)

(**MARK** *enters.*)

MARK. Well, he promoted Jay

TANIA. What?

Really?

MARK. And I'm laid off

    (beat)

TANIA. But you were the reason he…

MARK. I know I was the asshole who actually liked his job

TANIA. Oh God

Oh God

Oh no

Is it because you're coked up?

MARK. No, he didn't even notice.

We've lost our biggest client –

TANIA. Oh shit

NOVA?

MARK. Yeah

Yeah

A former employee dished some dirt to Travis

And they decided to dump us

And now he has to scale back

Harold's only keeping a few management positions

Jun Suk's a designer, he actually does something they
    need him

TANIA. Oh my god

MARK. Effective today

TANIA. What?

MARK. I guess they're afraid of us flipping out

TANIA. Us?

MARK. Yeah, it's a massacre

    (TANIA's phone beeps.)

TANIA. Oh shit.

MARK. No, don't worry they can't let you go

You're like the heart of this place

TANIA. *(to the phone)* Hey Harold.

Yeah, yeah.

I'll be right there.

MARK. Don't sweat it

(beat)

*(***TANIA*** exits.)*

*(***MARK*** calls his mom.)*

Hey mom,

Good, everything's good.

Yeah it turns out I'm coming back out this weekend

I know isn't that great

And um I can actually stay for a while

Yeah I'm gonna stay for a while and help you out with
the

No no mom I want to I have some extra time and I

I saw how much help you guys need out there so it's

All working out perfectly

How are you feeling?

Ok good well tell Jake I'm coming will you

Yup

I know me too.

*(He hangs up. Suddenly he kicks ***TANIA****'s desk. He stubs
his toe.)*

(He exits.)

*(After a moment, ***TANIA*** returns.)*

TANIA. Unbelievable.

They're giving my job to a fucking

*(She looks around and notices that ***MARK*** is not there.)*

(She exits.)

(She comes back with a box.)

(She starts packing things into the box.)

(She freezes.)

(She stands still for a moment, concentrating.)

(She looks around to make sure no one is around and then very quickly she slides her hand under her skirt and into her underwear.)

(She pulls her hand out and looks at it.)

TANIA. *(cont.)* Shit oh shit oh no oh shit

(She runs to the bathroom.)

(The phone starts ringing.)

(And ringing.)

(And ringing.)

(It finally stops.)

*(**TANIA** comes back in.)*

(She goes to her desk.)

*(**AMELIA** enters.)*

TANIA. *(cont.)* Nice boots

AMELIA. Yeah they're new I got paid for my
For Jun Suk.

TANIA. Wow he pays well.

AMELIA. I mean NYU paid me but
He left me a message
He killed it right?
He left me a message that just said
I Killed it!

TANIA.
Yeah yeah he did
he killed it   **AMELIA.**
apparently   Yes!
I wasn't there

AMELIA. I knew it! So they're not laying him off?

TANIA. No, no he got promoted.

(beat)

*(**AMELIA** screams.)*

TANIA. *(cont.)* Hey shhhhhh come on

AMELIA. That's amazing though isn't it amazing?!
  Can I see him

TANIA. Yeah
  Go on back I don't give a shit

  (TANIA buzzes the door.)

AMELIA. Hey also
  Do you want to go get our drink tonight

TANIA. Uh

AMELIA. I'm free this weekend
  Or next week or whatever
  Here's my card

TANIA. You have a card?

AMELIA. Yes, I went to this Seminar last night
  And I got inspired

TANIA. Wow

AMELIA. I got them made this morning right after I got Jun
  Suk's message
  I mean it seems like I'm good at this corporate
  coaching thing
  Right?
  And with all the layoffs
  People really need help with their presentations

TANIA. …Right

AMELIA. Hey could I have your cell number too?

TANIA. Oh
  I have your card

  (long Beat.)

  (TANIA takes out her phone.)

  646-458-0221

  (AMELIA dials the number. TANIA's phone rings, she answers it.)

AMELIA. Great we'll go get our drink!
Or I was even thinking
I read about this place The Popover Café
On the Upper West Side
You can share a big basket of Popovers
With jam and butter
And then maybe
We could go to Barney's after and just
Like look around

TANIA. I don't want to go to Barney's
No
I uh
I just got laid off

AMELIA. What

TANIA. Yeah they're scaling back
Even more
And a whole bunch of us
Got laid off
Me
Mark…

AMELIA. Mark? Why?

TANIA. I really don't know Amelia

AMELIA. Oh god I'm so sorry
Oh no
What about the…

(beat)

TANIA. Weirdly
It turns out I was just really really late so

AMELIA. …You guys could always try again

TANIA. I don't know if that's how it works in a situation like
this

(beat)

AMELIA. Listen

I know it feels terrible

Now

But something really wonderful will come out of this

TANIA. …

AMELIA. I mean you're too good for this job

Right?

And

Now

I mean yes it sucks

But now anything is possible

Who knows what you could do

You could make a whole new / life

TANIA. You know what it's late

and I have to pack up my shit so I should

You can go on back to see Jun Suk

(She holds the buzzer down.)

AMELIA. Oh ok hey I'm sorry

*(**TANIA** keeps pressing the buzzer until **AMELIA** has no choice but to exit.)*

I'm sorry if I

*(**TANIA** keeps buzzing.)*

*(**AMELIA** exits.)*

(beat)

*(**MARK** enters holding the box with all of his things.)*

MARK. You're kidding me

(He stops for a moment and starts rifling through one of his boxes.)

TANIA. Do you need help

MARK. No

Thanks

I know I packed it.

Now I just can't…
Huh.

TANIA. What will you do now?

MARK. Oh
Uh
I guess I'll go back to California for a while
Take care of my mom
I figure I might as well make the most of being
unemployed

TANIA. By taking care of your mom?

MARK. Well
Yeah

(**MARK** *starts digging in the box again.*)

Where the fuck is it
I'll probably find it like ten years from now
In a pocket or I don't know

TANIA. I used to have this skirt in high school
Every time I put it on, I found a dollar in the pocket
It was my magic skirt

MARK. Ha

(*beat*)

TANIA. I'm leaving too.

MARK. Oh yeah?

(**MARK**'s *phone is ringing.*)

TANIA. It's…
Untenable
don't you think?
Life here.

MARK. Working for these douche bags, fuck yeah

(**MARK** *hits ignore on his phone.*)

TANIA. Yeah, or even just living in this city.
Making a life in this city.
Might be untenable

MARK. Yeah

> (**MARK**'s *phone rings again.*)

> I uh

> I should probably take this so…

TANIA. Good luck to you

MARK. Oh yeah. You too, Tania

> I really liked working with you

> *(He answers the phone on his way out.)*

> Hey

> Yeah it's cool I already talked to her.

> Yeah

> *(His voice disappears along the hallway.)*

> *(The phone rings.)*

TANIA. Sutton, Feingold and McGrath.

> No she doesn't work here anymore.

> No I'm sorry.

> I'm sorry I don't know what to tell you.

> *(She starts to cry.)*

> What? No she's not coming back

> No no I'm fine I'm just sad because

> She was a really great employee

> *(She hangs and tries not to sob, gripping onto the desk with both hands.)*

> *(Then she wipes her face with tissues.)*

> *(The desk phone starts ringing. It rings and rings.)*

> *(After a moment it stops and* **TANIA**'s *cell phone goes off.)*

> Hello?

> What?

> Why are you calling my cell?

> Hey calm down what

> No, no don't give him water

Just sit him up so he doesn't choke
I'll call 911

(She hangs up. She calls 911.)

I need an ambulance at 9 Park Avenue
There's a man I think it's
Alcohol poisoning he's unconscious
No, no he's not homeless he's been promoted
It's 9 Park Avenue between 32nd and 33rd, second
    floor
I don't know I'm not with him

(She begins to exit.)

(Her voice trails off until she is gone.)

What yes, yes, ok
I'm going to him now
I'm walking toward him now

(As she walks toward JUN SUK the lobby of Sutton, Feingold and McGrath transforms into:)

SATURDAY, FEBRUARY 28

(JUN SUK's hospital room.)

(JUN SUK is asleep in his hospital bed.)

(There is an amazing view of the river from his window. It's as if we are in paradise.)

(AMELIA sits next to his bed.)

(After a moment, she looks down at her new boots and is filled with shame.)

(She tries to hide them, tucking her legs underneath her chair.)

(She looks around the room.)

(The room is filled with light.)

AMELIA. It's kind of

It feels kind of nice in here

(She looks at JUN SUK.)

When I first started teaching English I felt so useful.

Helping people make a new life is thrilling – even when it's hard it's still a new life

And sometimes I would think about my great great grandmother

who came to this country from Sweden.

A lot of people are like

why would anyone ever want to leave Sweden

but there was a time when a lot of people in Sweden were starving

and so my great great grandmother came to this country

and for a while she was really happy

but then she turned thirty-three and something happened:

Maybe she drank some bad well water or

maybe she was just lonely nobody knows

But apparently she started pasting drawings and
　　pictures
Of Sweden up all over her walls
and then after a while she wouldn't leave the house
she would just sit and stare at the pictures
So they locked her up at Western State Mental Hospital
in Tacoma, Washington and that's where she died
And since nobody could ever figure out what was
　　actually wrong with her
they listed the cause of death as Melancholia
So when I was teaching English I liked to imagine that
　　I was teaching somebody's future
great great grandmother
That maybe if there had been someone like me
To welcome her or
I don't know
I'm sorry
I'm sorry
I'm sorry I don't know how to help you

(**TANIA** *walks in. She is holding a bouquet of pink roses.*)

TANIA. How did you get in?

AMELIA. I'm his sister.

TANIA. Nice.

I'm his second wife.
His first wife will be here later
Their kid's in a show tonight
She sounded so sad

(*She holds up the roses.*)

Do these look ok?:
Pink is for newborns but it's all they had
Can you help me make them into one big bouquet?
I think that will look nicer

AMELIA. Oh I don't have a lot of talent for this type of

(**TANIA** *has unwrapped the paper.*)

TANIA. I'll just take the plastic off and then put them
    Together in the paper
    Here I got this extra paper can you hold it

AMELIA. Sure

TANIA. Ok now just spread it out on the table and I'll lay
    these out

(She is separating the roses)

Should I lay them down straight or diagonal do you
    think?

AMELIA. Uh

TANIA. We should do this together.

AMELIA. Ok well then I like diagonal.

TANIA. No I don't think that will look good.

(TANIA lays the roses down, very carefully one by one.)

Will you get the tissue paper out of that bag?

(AMELIA opens the bag.)

Can you lay the tissue paper down.

(AMELIA does this. TANIA looks at it for a moment.)

Actually I think you're right diagonal could look nice.

(She lays the roses down diagonally.)

Yeah.

(She wraps them up in the paper.)

Can you hand me that rubber band?

(AMELIA does)

(TANIA wraps it around the stems.)

The rubber band looks kind of shitty right?

AMELIA. Maybe

(AMELIA picks up some of the tissue paper.)

(She folds it several times into a long band.)

*(She puts the tissue paper band around the rubber band,
covering it.)*

TANIA. You gave it a belt!

> (**AMELIA** *rips a little piece of tape with her teeth and tapes the belt.*)

> Nice work.

AMELIA. Yeah
> I like it too.

> *(pause)*

> What do we do now

TANIA. …I think we just wait for him to wake up

> *(long Pause)*

> *(softly)* Hey Jun Suk
> Wake up
> we're here
> We're right here

AMELIA. …Your sister and your second wife

TANIA. See what surprises are in store for you?

AMELIA. Who knows what else could happen
> So much is possible

TANIA. All kinds of miracles
> Are just

> *(They stand by* **JUN SUK**'s *bed.)*

End of Play